THE Curious Explorer's GUIDE TO THE MOOMINHOUSE

THE Moominhouse

THE MOOMINHOUSE

Welcome to Moominvalley! At the valley's very heart stands the **MOOMINHOUSE** – the wonderful home of the generous and hospitable *Finn Family Moomin*. One of their many guests is hurrying up the verandah steps right now, look! It's Little My, come to show *Moomintroll* her brand new umbrella.

T̲H̲E̲ DRAWING-ROOM

In the drawing-room, where the family sits down to
Moominmamma's delicious, stove-cooked meals,
Little My finds Sniff, who is finishing a late breakfast.
She asks if he has seen *Moomin*, but Sniff's mouth
is full of syrupy pancake. Before he can reply,
    Little My hears cheerful **HUMMING**,
        and goes to investigate . . .

THE CELLAR

Down in the cool, earthy cellar, *Moominmamma* is fetching a fresh pot of damson jam. She keeps all kinds of **PROVISIONS** stored down here – from bottled raspberry juice, to pine needles, to tummy powder (in case of emergency).

She suggests to Little My that *Moomin* is perhaps spending the morning with Snorkmaiden.

THE
STAIRCASE

Little My scampers up the staircase, nodding to the faded portraits of *Moomin* family ancestors. On the landing above, the Hemulen is just coming out of his guest-room door all set for a morning's **INSECT** collecting.

THE ROOM FOR EVERYTHING

Across the landing, Little My notices that the door to the Room For Everything is ajar. She peeps inside. It isn't *Moomin*, however, who is rooting through the **WONDERFUL CLUTTER** within. It's Thingumy and Bob – 'trooking for leasure', they tell Little My. She leaves them to it, and hurries on to Snorkmaiden's room.

SNORKMAIDEN'S ROOM

Snorkmaiden is at her vanity table, trying to settle on the best
HEADWEAR for a fine summer's day like today – and finding
it very difficult. She hasn't seen *Moomintroll* since breakfast.
Snorkmaiden wonders, as she considers her favourite sparkly tiara,
if Little My might find him
in his bedroom.

MOOMIN'S ROOM

There is no sign of *Moomin* in his room, but Little My spots the ROPE LADDER dangling from the windowsill, and suspects that *Moomin* may have climbed out of the window. If he is outdoors, Little My knows just the place from which to spot him. She hurries off, up to the attic at the very top of the Moominhouse.

THE GARDEN

From the rooftop **WINDOW**, Little My can see everything down in the sun-warmed garden below – the *Moominhouse's* garden, with *Moominmamma's* beautiful rose-beds, and *Moominpappa's* woodshed...

...and *Moomintroll!*
He is down at the forest edge,
watching the hot air balloons with
his best friend Snufkin.

MOOMINPAPPA'S <u>STUDY</u>

As Little My rushes back downstairs,
Moominpappa huffs in his study chair.
This is *Moominpappa's* private place. He
comes here to think, write poetry, or work
on his adventure-packed MEMOIRS. He is
finding it rather hard to concentrate with
all Little My's rushing to and fro.

TROPICAL
SEEDS

HOW
TO
BE
HAPPY

HOW
TO
BE
CON

THE VERANDAH

Little My hurries off to show Moomin her new umbrella. Even as she leaves the Moominhouse, more VISITORS are calling by, sure of finding whatever comfort they seek – a slice of plum cake, a sympathetic ear, or a bed for the night – in the warm and welcoming home of the *Finn Family Moomin*.

THE END